Helen Orme taught for many years before giving up teaching to write full-time. At the last count she had written over 70 books.

She writes both fiction and non-fiction, but at present is concentrating on fiction for older readers.

Helen also runs writing workshops for children and courses for teachers in both primary and secondary schools.

How many have you read?

Brother Bother

Helen Orme

Ransom

Brother Bother

by Helen Orme
Illustrated by Cathy Brett
Cover by Anna Torborg

Published by Ransom Publishing Ltd.
51 Southgate Street, Winchester, Hants. SO23 9EH
www.ransom.co.uk

ISBN   978 184167 684 5

First published in 2007

Meet the Sisters ...

Siti and her friends are really close. So close she calls them her Sisters. They've been mates for ever, and most of the time they are closer than her real family.

Siti is the leader – the one who always knows what to do – but Kelly, Lu, Donna and Rachel have their own lives to lead as well.

Still, there's no one you can talk to, no one you can rely on, like your best mates. Right?

1

I don't believe you!

"Mum," Siti called as she went in through the kitchen door.

There was no answer. Mum must still be at work. Hanif and Afia would still be with the childminder, but Daudi should be home by now.

She went upstairs to Daudi's room and walked in.

"Get out!" he yelled, grabbing his school bag.

As he grabbed the bag, a small plastic pack fell out onto the floor.

"What's that?" asked Siti.

"Mind your own … – nothing to do with you!"

He grabbed for the pack, but Siti was quicker.

She looked at it – it was an MP3 player.

"Where did you get this?" she asked.

"Bought it," said Daudi sulkily.

"No you didn't – you don't have that kind of money."

"It was in the sale."

"Don't believe you!"

Daudi grabbed for it again. "It's mine. Give it back."

"Tell me where you got it, then."

Daudi glared at Siti. He sat down on his bed and folded his arms.

"You know Dad said you couldn't have one," said Siti. "Tell me where it came from."

Daudi just sat on his bed. He didn't move. He didn't say anything.

"O.K.," said Siti. "I'll wait 'til Dad gets home and tell him."

"No," said Daudi. "He'll go mad."

"So tell me, then."

Daudi pulled a face. He looked as if he was going to cry. "It wasn't my fault! They made me do it."

2

Bunking off

Siti sat down on the bed next to Daudi. "Come on, tell me."

Daudi began to explain. He and Jason had skipped the last lesson at school.

"Dad'll go mad when they tell him," said Siti.

"He won't know. Miss Harper was off sick. We had some dozy supply teacher. We saw him going into the maths room, so we bunked off."

They had caught the bus to the shopping centre and gone to the library to use the computers there. Then they'd met some older boys who were friends with Jason's brother. The boys had started teasing Jason and Daudi.

Daudi, who hated being teased, got wound up, and when one of the boys called him a little brat – that had been it!

Danny had given them a mouthful of abuse. The biggest of the boys, Aaron, had grabbed him and threatened to beat him up.

Jason tried to help, but the boys said they would only let Daudi go if he could show them he was as clever as he said he was.

Aaron said that they got loads of stuff from the shops by nicking it, and that if Daudi was that clever, he had to go into a shop and nick something without being caught.

"You prat!" said Siti. "You know better than that."

"I know. I just got really mad."

3

"It's got to go back"

"How did you get it? They keep these things locked up. Why didn't it set off the alarms?"

"Some guy was looking at loads of them. They had got them all over the counter. When they went to look at some other stuff, I just grabbed it."

"But what about the door alarm?"

Daudi grinned. "That was clever," he said. "I put it in my bag and then just kicked the bag out of the door. It went under the alarm so nothing happened."

"What happened then?" she asked.

"When I got out, they'd all legged it – even Jason," he said. "So I just came home."

"You've got to take it back," said Siti. "If you explain, they might not be too cross."

"I can't," said Daudi. He looked really upset. "Dad said he'd stop my pocket money for a month if I got into trouble again."

"Well it's got to go back," said Siti. "If you're too scared, I'll do it. I'll just take it back in and put it back on one of the shelves. Maybe they'll think it just fell down."

4

The alarm

Siti scribbled a quick note for her mum and they left for the bus stop. It was getting quite late by the time they got to the shopping centre.

They got to the shop.

"You wait here," said Siti. "It'll only take me a couple of minutes."

She went in through the door. But then the terrible thing happened. The alarm went off.

Siti hadn't realised that it happened when you went in through the door as well as when you came out.

A man came towards her.

"What's going on?" he asked. "Why did the alarm go off?"

Siti looked around – could she make a run for it? No, that would be silly.

"I think I've got something of yours," she said.

"It seems like it," said the man. "You'd better come and see the manager."

He took her through a door at the end of the shop. A young woman was sitting at a desk.

"This girl set the door alarm off," he said. "She says she's got something of ours."

"Well," said the woman, looking hard at Siti. "Would you like to tell me what's going on?"

Siti took the MP3 player from her pocket.

"I think this is yours," she said.

5

"I didn't steal anything!"

"How did you get it?" asked the woman. "I have to tell you, we always get the police in for shoplifters."

Siti stared at her in horror.

"But I didn't steal anything. I was coming *into* the shop, not trying to take it out!"

The woman might have been young, but she was hard. She looked at Siti without smiling.

"Tell me," she demanded.

Siti thought fast. What was she going to say? She couldn't tell on Daudi.

She didn't know what to say. Maybe the best thing would be to keep quiet.

"I found it. I knew it came from here. I brought it back."

"Where did you 'find' it?"

Siti shook her head. That was all she was going to say.

The woman looked as if she was getting angry.

"I don't know what you lot are up to this time," she said. "But I've had enough of you and your gang. We've got you and it's the police this time."

She got up from her chair and spoke, quietly, to the guy. He went back into the shop.

She sat down again and looked at Siti.

"You're in big trouble this time, lady," she said. "They have promised that they will prosecute next time we catch anyone."

"But I didn't steal anything!" Siti was really worried now and she almost shouted at the woman. "It wasn't me!"

6

"Save it for the police"

"Save it for the police," said the woman. "They'll be here soon."

Siti just sat. There was no point in saying any more. What would she tell the police? What would they do to her? Would they believe her?

Anything she said would get Daudi into trouble. Daudi! What was he doing now?

She felt so bad. It was stupid to have tried to bring it back. She should have just left it alone.

There was a sharp knock on the door. The police. Already!

The door opened and in came …

"Dad!"

Mr Musa smiled at Siti, then he smiled at the woman.

"Hello Marcie. How are you?"

To Siti's surprise the woman smiled back at her dad.

"Hello sir."

"I've come to explain what happened," said Siti's dad. "I hope you'll believe what I say."

Marcie nodded, and smiled again.

Mr Musa sat down.

"I'm here because my son rang me and told me all about it. Siti really was trying to bring the MP3 player back."

He explained the whole thing to the woman. Siti couldn't think of her as Marcie.

He'd just finished when the police arrived, so he had to start all over again.

Daudi was brought in and had to listen to some straight talking from everybody. But in the end everyone believed that he wasn't part of the gang.

The policeman was even quite pleased in the end, because Daudi was able to give him some names.

But he was very stern with Daudi.

"We'll be keeping a close eye on that little lot," he said. "But you stay away from them in future."

"I'll make sure of that," said Dad. "You were lucky that they believed what you had to say, otherwise you would have been in a lot of trouble. And not just with the police."

At last, they were all allowed to leave. Daudi wasn't very happy: he still had to face Dad at home.

"How did you know the manager?" asked Siti.

"I taught her, years ago," said Dad. "She was one of my best pupils, but I did have a go at her once, for telling lies. I think that's why you got off so lightly," he added, looking at Daudi.

"Good thing you came to the rescue, Dad! You did better than Siti."

Siti had only one thing to say to him. She glared at him, trying to remember Marcie's glare.

"Bother brothers!"